Let's Play

SMILE!

Written and illustrated by
BreNda E. Koch

This is ME.

 Did you Laugh ?

When we are BORN,
we are

all

BABIES.

We May LOOK The Same, BUT we are NOT. FROM The COLOUR OF OUR SKiN TO The Shape OF OUR BODies, we aRe aLL

DIFFERENT.

SOMe OF US

have ROUNd heads

SOMe OF US

DON'T.

SOME OF US have TWO eyes SOME OF US DON'T.

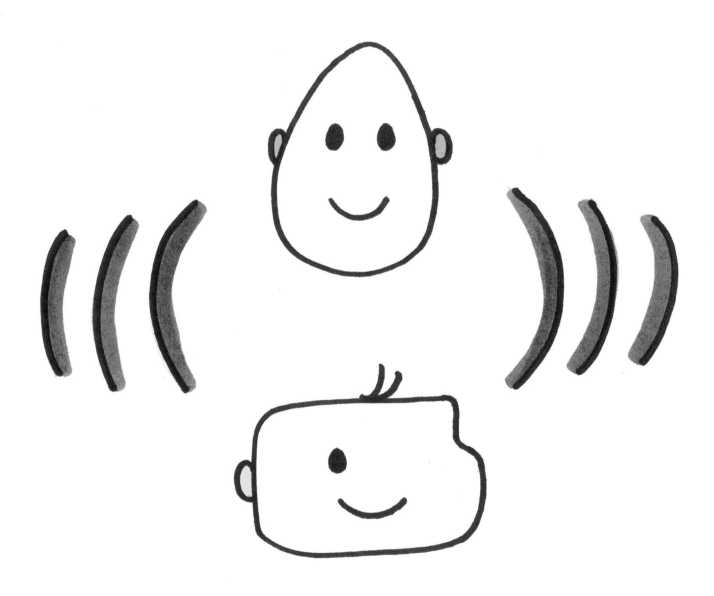

SOMe OF US have
((((TWO eaRS
SOMe OF US)))
DON'T.

Some of us have 2 arms, 2 hands, 2 legs and 2 feet

SOME OF US
DON'T.

SOME OF US
CAN WALK.

Some of us CAN'T.

SOME OF US
CAN SEE,

SOME OF US
CAN'T.

We are all
DIFFERENT.

We are NOT BROKEN, we are UNIQUE.

We all do things differently. We are UNIQUE.

LOOK what we CAN DO, NOT what we caN'T do .

We are perfect just the way we are. We are UNIQUE!

Hi, I'm Bobby and this is me. I like TRUCKS, BLOCKS, painting and reading. LET'S PLAY!!!!!

About the Author

Educated as an Aboriginal Child Development Practitioner and Early Childhood Educator, Brenda E. Koch has worked and volunteered with children for over thirty years.

For most of her life, Brenda's mother (who was diagnosed with multiple sclerosis when Brenda was just a little girl) lived in a hospital. During their many visits, Brenda found herself becoming increasingly aware of how people with disabilities are viewed by others. That awareness was the inspiration for Let's Play!, and with it, she hopes to nurture an appreciation and understanding of our differences, as well as our similarities.

Currently living in Ontario, Canada, Brenda enjoys spending time with her family. She can often be found swimming at the YMCA and biking with her dog Kilo.

Let's Play! is Brenda's debut published work and the first in a series of books for young children. Coming soon, from Brenda E. Koch: Let's Go!

 FriesenPress

Suite 300 - 990 Fort St
Victoria, BC, V8V 3K2
Canada

www.friesenpress.com

ISBN
978-1-5255-3973-2 (Hardcover)
978-1-5255-3974-9 (Paperback)
978-1-5255-3975-6 (eBook)

1. JUVENILE FICTION

Distributed to the trade by The Ingram Book Company

CPSIA information can be obtained
at www.ICGtesting.com
Printed in the USA
LVHW072103250219
608724LV00001B/2/P

9 781525 539749